VINCENT THE ARTIST BOOKS
Published by 19th Day Pictures Press
ISBN-13: 978-0692452394 (19th Day Press)
19th Day Press Books for Young Readers
PO Box 17512, Encino, California 91416, U.S.A

First published by 19th Day Press 2015

ISBN-10: 0692452397
Library of Congress Book One registration 2015: CS#1-2307920875
Library of Congress Original Character registration 2004: VAu000608897
Library of Congress Original Screenplay registration 2004: TXu001202752
WGA Original Screenplay renewed registration 2012: 1568148

Manufactured in the United States of America

Dedicated to Vincent Van Gogh and his Brilliant Works of Art

Self-Portrait in Front of the Easel
Paris, early 1888
Oil on canvas

One beautiful evening off in the distance, there appeared several colorful hot-air balloons that drifted across the summer sky.

Confetti-like scrap paper spilled out of the balloon's basket, raining down over the quilted landscape, announcing that the Traveling Cirque D' Amour had come to town.

One piece of scrap paper in particular looped and danced along the swirling breeze as it passed the countryside filled with vibrant green and violet hues reminding us of Vincent Van Gogh's *Couples in the Voyer d'Argenson Park at Asnières*.

Couples in the Voyer d'Argenson Park at Asnières

Paris, June-July 1887 - Oil on canvas

by Vincent Van Gogh

The playful, gentle wind carried the paper high, high, then higher above Harvard school's entrance, over the walls and past dozens of children on their way to class.

The breeze dipped and the paper buckled, dropping without rhyme or reason toward the ground, magically wriggling its way through a storm drain as it traveled downward into...

... the sewer below, curling through a dazzling subterranean world...

... illuminated only by an earthly light from above.

Then once again it caught flight before riding upon a flurry of air, past a stunningly handsome bridge that only a great artist could bring to life.

The Langlois Bridge at Arles

Arles, 1888 - Oil on canvas

by Vincent Van Gogh

The paper's promise of circus games, fantastic feats and daredevil tricks rose up over the entrance of a magnificent underground city before it swiftly plummeted down, down, down...

... then after colliding with a lamppost only to change direction...

... the paper whipped, whisked and wound its way over a small footbridge.

As if it was meant to be, the paper jetted in through Vincent's open bedroom window...

... as he was hard at work finishing his latest work of art which looked eerily familiar to Vincent Van Gogh's *Wheat Field with Crows*.

Wheat Field with Crows

Auvers-sur-Oise, July 1890 - Oil on canvas

by Vincent Van Gogh

Vincent read the Cirque D' Amour's enchanting message of new and exciting experiences, worldly adventures and the allure of destinations unknown. A perfect antidote for a young aspiring artist.

That night at dinner Vincent planned on telling his family about his dream of being a great artist.

He waited for just the right moment. But before he could open his
mouth...

... Vincent's father had an announcement. *"Oh Vincent, I have
wonderful news. I've made all the necessary arrangements for you to
begin your teaching career right here with me at Harvard Ground
School. Isn't that lovely?"*

This news upset Vincent so much that he leapt to his feet and shouted, "NO! I WANT TO BE AN ARTIST!"

You can just imagine Professor Van Raatt's reaction to Vincent's shocking news.

Even Grandma Hummy murmured in disbelief... *"Trouble, trouble, trouble."*

Vincent knew he had no other choice but to follow his heart. Early the next morning he popped open a manhole cover and peered out from below, getting his first glimpse of the above-ground human world.

So with a mighty push he tossed the heavy sewer lid off and climbed out.

Vincent gathered up his suitcase, drawing pad and artist supplies then set out on his journey to be a great artist.

Vincent heard the whistle of a train off in the distance. Following the sound, he disappeared into a dark, avocado-green field, reminiscent of Vincent Van Gogh's *Farmhouse in a Wheat Field*.

Farmhouse in a Wheat Field

Arles, May 1888 - Oil on Canvas

by Vincent Van Gogh

Vincent arrived at the train station through a maze of hidden tunnels and passage ways. Through a small opening in the wall he could see the giant feet of the humans his grandmother had warned him about.

Vincent bravely poked his head out from the tiny hole in the wall to scan the station for a safe path through the giant people who loomed above him.

Vincent was so small compared to the oversized humans moving around him, he felt almost invisible.

But not too small to go unnoticed by the notorious Bounty Cat, a virile, feral cat who lived to devour creatures just like Vincent.

Vincent planned to dash through the maze of travelers with a zig and a zag, a glide and a slide and a twist and a twirl, hoping to safely arrive at the small rat-hole opening across the station that would lead him to the Rat Depot entrance.

So with a dart he was off, holding on tight to both suitcases. Vincent ran the gauntlet of human travelers.

After marking Vincent as his next meal, the hideous Bounty Cat struck with fury. From behind a wall he sprang out in hot pursuit.

The chase was on. Vincent ran for his life. He zigged when Bounty Cat zagged. Vincent jumped high into the air as Bounty Cat pounced low, missing the little fellow as Vincent sped off, running faster and faster and even faster.

Bounty Cat let out a terrifying roar. The wild beast was on the loose and right behind Vincent.

Closer and closer, faster and faster, then bigger than life, Bounty Cat pounced.

Vincent scampered for his life, racing toward the nearest exit.

With a nasty thwack Bounty Cat tore open Vincent's suitcase, barely missing young Vincent.

Chug-a-chug-a-chug... moving down the track the train barreled into the station.

With a powerful swipe Bounty Cat swung his sharp claws at Vincent but the little artist dodged the blows once again as he leapt high into the air.

It looked like certain peril for Vincent as the locomotive headed straight for him.

As young Vincent gracefully glided across the train track and out of reach of the notorious Bounty Cat, he was heard to say, *"Aaah, an artist's life. Man, I just knew it would be exciting."*